# THE LITTLE PRINCESS
# OF TAPPINTOE

# THE LITTLE PRINCESS OF TAPPINTOE

by

P.J. Meltabarger

Illustrated by Shelly Witschorke

F
Mel    Meltabarger, P.J.
        The Little Princess of Tappintoe, by P.J. Meltabarger.
        Illus. by Shelly Witschorke.
        Ozark Publishing, Inc., 1995.
        27P. illus.
        Summary:  A princess and a horse.

ISBN Paperback   1-56763-174-6
ISBN Casebound 1-56763-175-4

Ozark Publishing, Inc.
P.O. Box 228
Prairie Grove, AR 72753
Ph: 1-800-321-5671

Printed in the United States of America

Dedicated to

all girls who are looking for a swan.

# THE LITTLE PRINCESS OF TAPPINTOE

$O$nce
upon a time
in the land
of Tappintoe,
there lived a little
princess named
Kimberli. She was a
very happy little princess
because her father, King Kuttarug,
always gave her everything that her heart desired.
Her wish was indeed a command in the land of Tappintoe!

One day, little Princess Kimberli asked her father, King Kuttarug, for a pony. And then, she smiled because she knew that her wish was a command in the land of Tappintoe.

Behold, within the hour, a beautiful, white, prancing pony was delivered to the palace gate. The steed was bedecked in blue and gold trappings that glistened beneath the rays of the warm, summer morn. Princess Kimberli squealed with delight at the beautiful sight, and she named him Pony Mahoney.

From that day forward, the people in the land of Tappintoe gathered in the town square to cheer as Princess Kimberli and Pony Mahoney appeared. And thus, the twosome came to be, a delightful and merry sight to see!

Many days passed
with Princess Kimberli
seated atop her dancing
and prancing Pony
Mahoney. They traversed
the land of Tappintoe,
picking pretty flowers in
the meadow. They frolicked
and raced across the grass.
She was indeed one happy lass!

Princess Kimberli and Pony Mahoney were content until the day that the little princess saw the swan quietly swimming upon the crystal blue surface of Lake Gotta-Lotta-Water. Then, she promptly dismounted Pony Mahoney and stared at the majestic white bird.

Princess Kimberli sighed, and then she cried, "Oh, my pretty Pony Mahoney, I must hurry home to tell my father that I must have a swan. Step lively, my steed. We must begone!"

Thus, the excited
princess and her prancing
Pony Mahoney raced back
to the palace to tell King
Kuttarug of her latest desire.
He listened and smiled as she
described the graceful white bird
gliding upon the crystal blue surface
of Lake Gotta-Lotta-Water.

Behold, within the hour, a messenger arrived at the palace gate. He was carrying a red velvet pillow in a gold chest. Princess Kimberli squealed with delight at the beautiful sight and ran to look inside.

But, alas, everyone gasped as she peeked within, for it was then she jumped back, and she cried with chagrin, "Oh, Father dear, what have you done? This is not a swan, but a duck who's no fun! His feathers are yellow. His feet are too big. His head is too little, and his bill a bent twig. Take him away!"

King Kuttarug smiled as he peered down at the frail little fellow seated upon the red velvet pillow. Then, His Majesty, the king, spoke a word that had never been heard throughout the land of Tappintoe. "No!"

The crowd gasped and groaned, taking heed. They knew that this day was a sad day indeed! As Princess Kimberli and Pony Mahoney turned to leave, an echo was heard of the forbidden word,

"No! no, no, no."

And a tear slowly slid down her cheek.

Many days passed, but nary one smile lightened the sorrow within the land of Tappintoe. Each day, the people spoke in a whisper as Princess Kimberli and her Pony Mahoney sadly traversed the kingdom. The little daughter of King Kuttarug and her Pony Mahoney no longer smiled or danced or pranced. They were indeed a sad sight to behold.

One day King Kuttarug sent a messenger to summon his daughter.

"Return to the palace at once!"

Princess Kimberli obeyed, even though her feelings were hurt from the king speaking that dreadful "No" word in her presence!

"Yes, Father, you wish to see me?"

"Yes, my daughter. Have you seen your swan who sits upon the red velvet pillow in the gold chest?"

"Oh no, Father!" she gasped. "I can not;
I will not look at the unsightly bird, for
there is no swan to see. He is but a
duck, and no fun will he be! His
feathers are yellow; his feet are
too big. His head is too little,
and his bill a bent twig!"

"I order you to go
now, my princess, and
look at your duck. You
may find that your little
yellow-feathered, big-footed,
little headed, bent billed duck
has changed!"

And thus, it came to pass in the land of Tappintoe, there lives little Princess Kimberli, Pony Mahoney, King Kuttarug, and a beautiful swan named Swash Buckle.  Princess Kimberli is very happy because her father always gives her anything that her heart desires, and her words are indeed a command in the land of Tappintoe.

## The moral to this story is:

Life may seem
A ducky bit bad
But do not fret
Nor feel too sad
For your duck may
One day
Be a Swan!